Illustrated by Art Mawhinney

Additional illustrations by the Disney Storybook Artists

Published by Louis Weber, C.E.O.
Publications International, Ltd.
7373 North Cicero Avenue, Lincolnwood, Illinois 60712
Ground Floor, 59 Gloucester Place, London W1U 8JJ

Customer Service: 1-800-595-8484
or customer_service@pilbooks.com

www.pilbooks.com

Manufactured in China.

p i kids is a registered trademark of Publications International, Ltd.
Look and Find is a registered trademark of Publications International, Ltd., in the United States and in Canada.

8 7 6 5 4 3 2 1

ISBN-13: 978-1-4127-9372-8
ISBN-10: 1-4127-9372-6

CALICO SENDS HIS HENCHMEN TO CAPTURE PENNY. LUCKILY, PENNY HAS HER DOG BOLT FOR PROTECTION. BOLT USES HIS SUPER STRENGTH, SUPER SPEED, AND POWERFUL SUPER BARK TO HELP PENNY ESCAPE. SEARCH FOR THESE BAD GUYS THAT BOLT BATTLES.

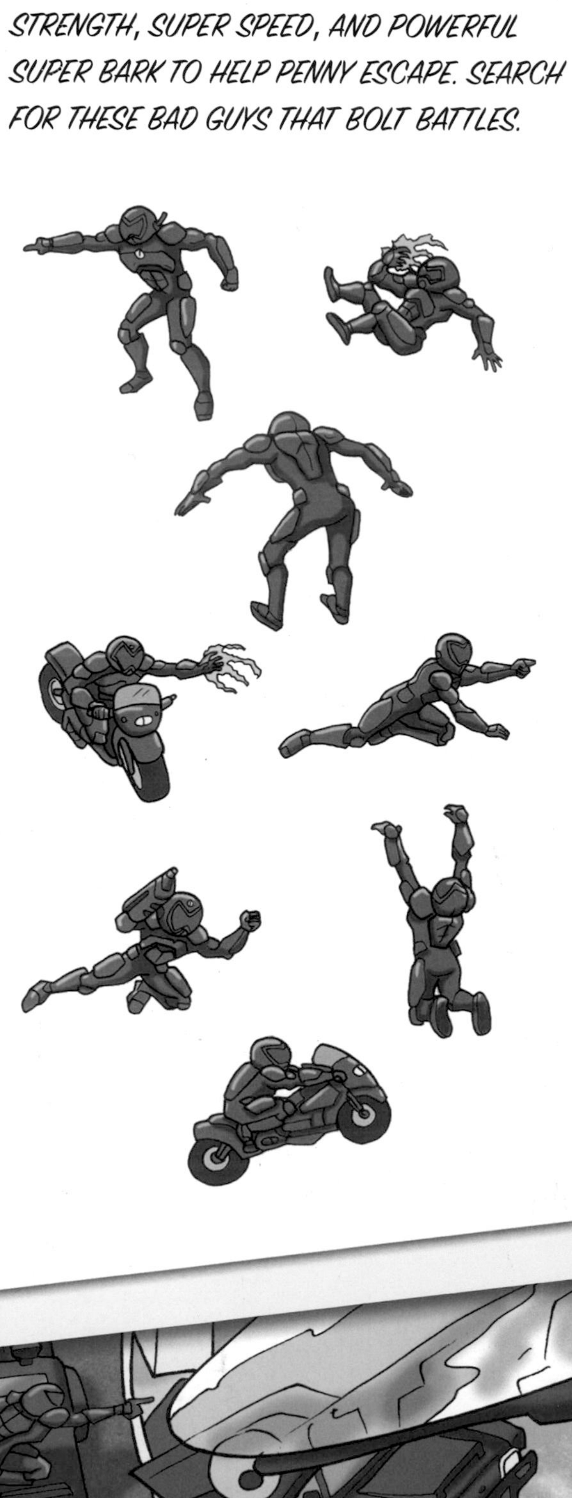

MILK
MILK

CALICO HAS CAPTURED PENNY! BOLT FRANTICALLY SEARCHES FOR HER, BUT HE CAN'T FIND HER ANYWHERE. AS BOLT RACES THROUGH THE STUDIO'S MAILROOM, HE ACCIDENTALLY SMACKS INTO A WINDOW...AND FALLS INTO A BOX THAT'S ABOUT TO BE SHIPPED! LOOK FOR THESE OTHER BOXES THAT WILL SOON BE SHIPPED.

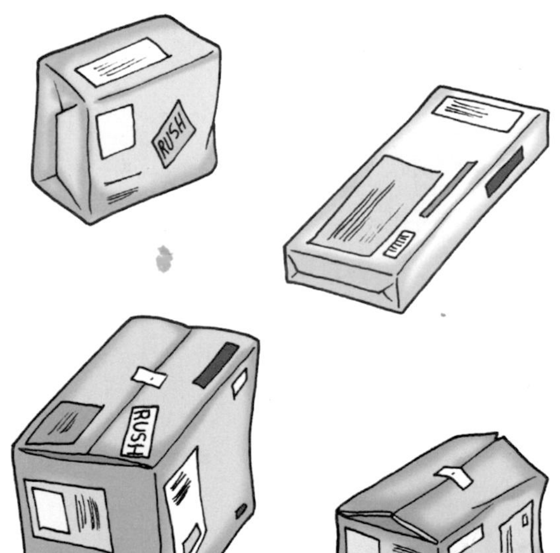

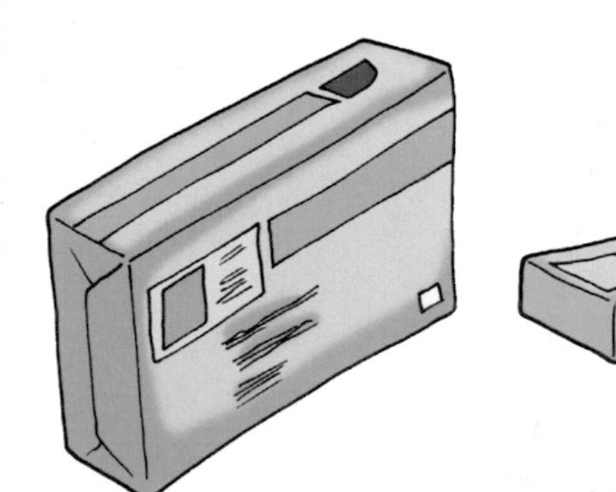

PRIORITY
RUSH
RUSH
SHIP TO NYC
PRIORITY
RUSH

WHEN BOLT FINALLY GETS FREE FROM THE BOX, HE FINDS HIMSELF IN THE MIDDLE OF NEW YORK CITY. HE RUNS THROUGH THE CROWDED STREETS, LOOKING FOR ANY SIGN OF PENNY...UNTIL HE GETS STUCK IN A PARK FENCE! FIND THESE PEOPLE WHO SAW BOLT ZOOM PAST.

TAXI
TAXI
TAXI
TAXI
TAXI
BOLT

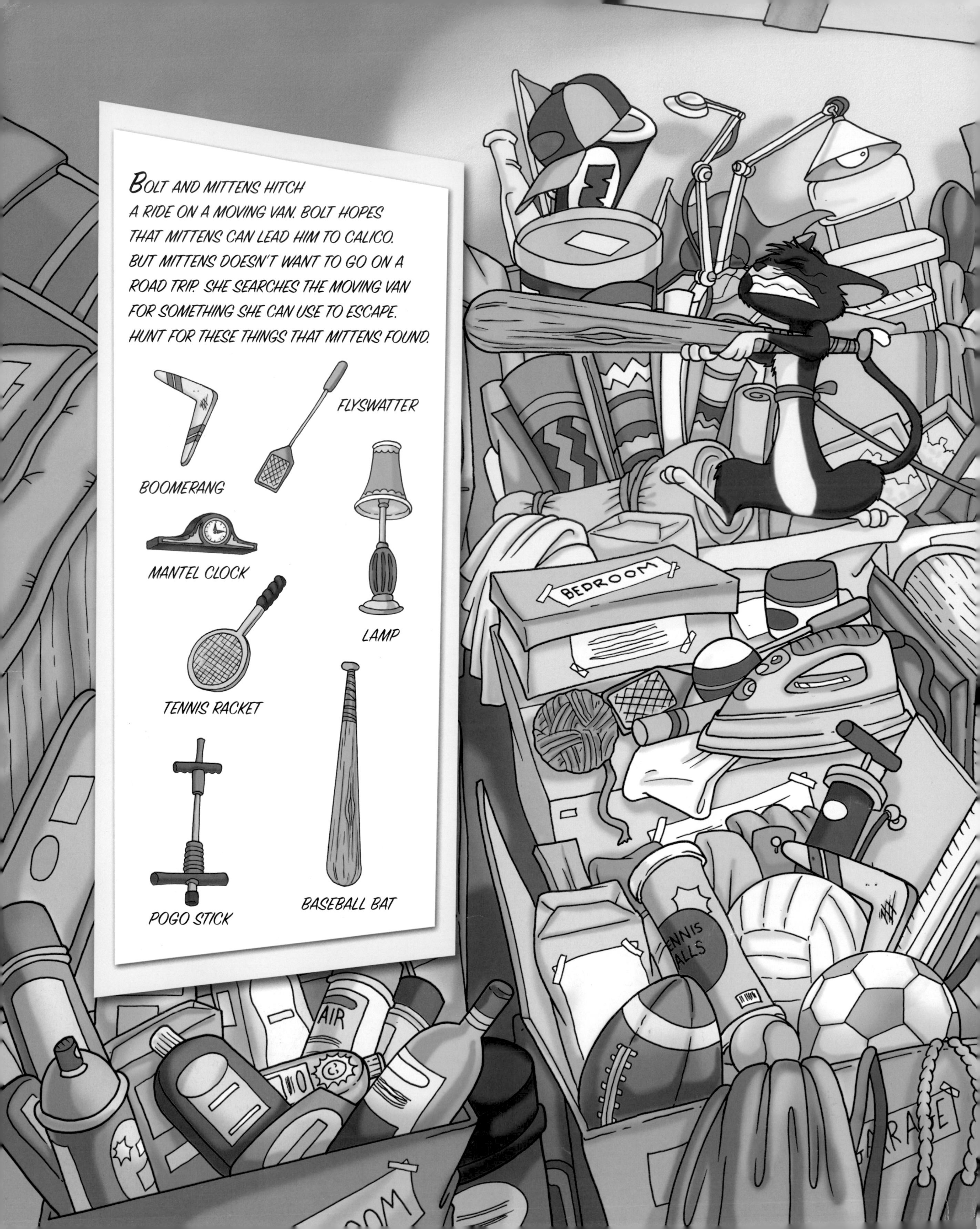
BOLT AND MITTENS HITCH A RIDE ON A MOVING VAN. BOLT HOPES THAT MITTENS CAN LEAD HIM TO CALICO. BUT MITTENS DOESN'T WANT TO GO ON A ROAD TRIP. SHE SEARCHES THE MOVING VAN FOR SOMETHING SHE CAN USE TO ESCAPE. HUNT FOR THESE THINGS THAT MITTENS FOUND.
BOOMERANG
FLYSWATTER
MANTEL CLOCK
LAMP
TENNIS RACKET
BASEBALL BAT
POGO STICK
BEDROOM
AIR
TENNIS BALLS
GARAGE

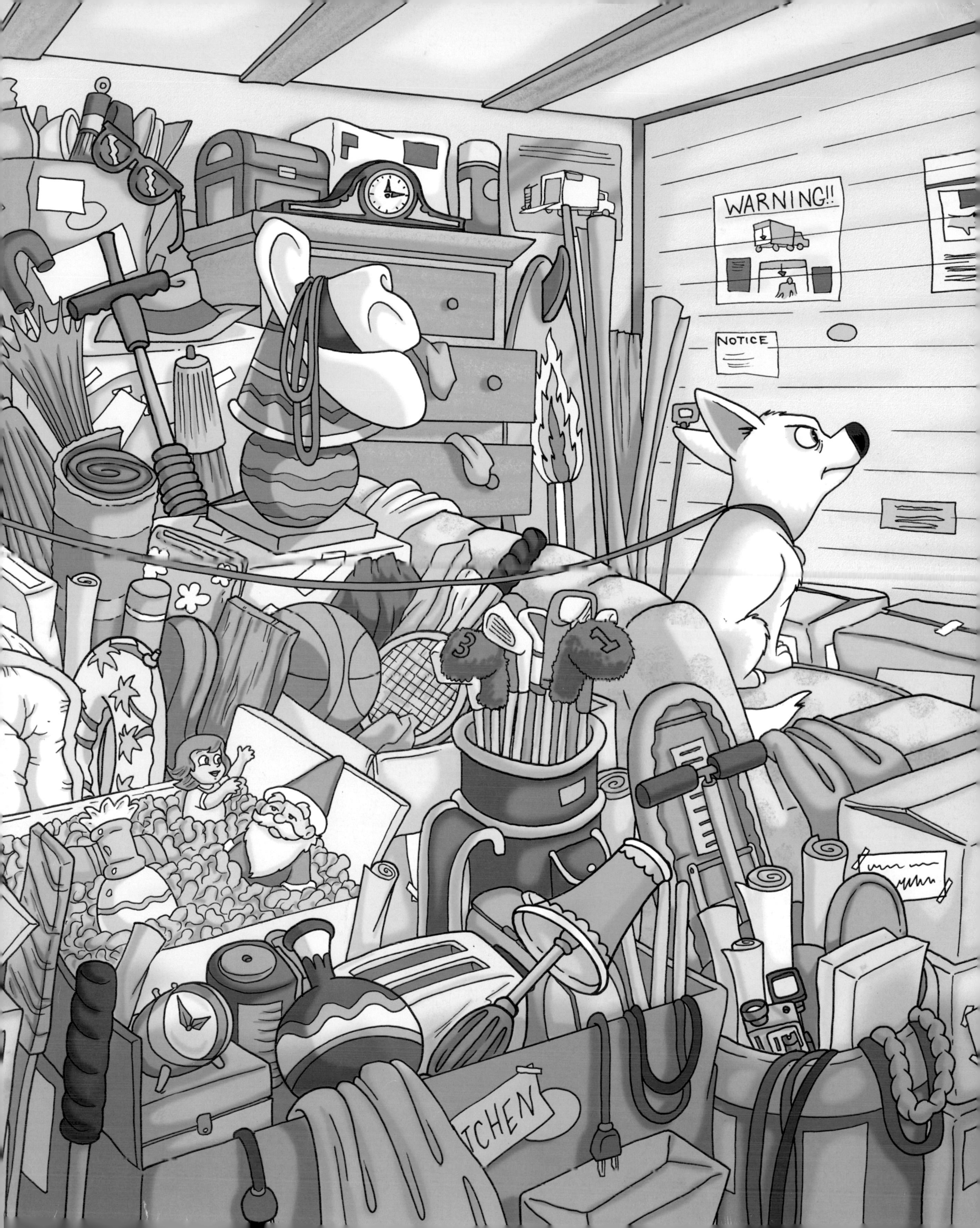
WARNING!!
NOTICE
TCHEN

BOLT AND MITTENS HAVE BEEN TRAVELING FOR A LONG TIME, AND THEY'RE FEELING VERY HUNGRY! THEY ARRIVE AT THE RV PARK JUST IN TIME FOR DINNER SCRAPS. LOOK AROUND THE PARK TO FIND THE BEST COOKS.

WHEN MITTENS GETS LOCKED UP IN THE POUND, BOLT AND RHINO GO ON A MISSION TO RESCUE HER. RHINO CREATES A NOISY DISTRACTION WHILE BOLT TRIES TO REACH MITTENS WITHOUT BEING DETECTED. LOOK FOR THESE DOGS BARKING OUT "BALL! BALL! BALL!"
CAT ROOM

PET ADOPTION WEEK

FIRE ON THE SET! BOLT GETS BACK TO THE STUDIO LOT JUST AS A FIRE STARTS ON THE SET OF THE TV SHOW. EVERYONE QUICKLY EVACUATES THE BUILDING. AMONG THE CROWD, FIND THESE PEOPLE WHO WORK WITH PENNY.
PENNY'S AGENT
DIRECTOR
PENNY'S HAIRDRESSER
NETWORK EXECUTIVE
MAKEUP ARTIST
PENNY'S STYLIST
THE PROFESSOR
5

4
BOL
WEEKLY
BULANCE

AFTER PENNY AND BOLT ARE REUNITED, THEY MOVE TO THE COUNTRY. THEY TAKE A BREAK FROM UNPACKING AND HAVE FUN PLAYING TOGETHER. LOOK FOR THESE TOYS THAT BELONG TO BOLT AND MITTENS.
DOG BONE
TOY MOUSE
BALL OF YARN
TUG TOY
BALL
FLYING DISK

BOLT ALWAYS LOOKS OUT FOR THE SAFETY OF INNOCENT BYSTANDERS. GO BACK TO THE CHASE SCENE AND FIND THESE VEHICLES THAT BOLT SEES ON THE FREEWAY.
SCHOOL BUS
PIZZA DELIVERY CAR
CONVERTIBLE
MINIVAN
PRODUCE TRUCK
TANKER TRUCK
NO ONE NOTICES BOLT AMONG ALL THE SHIPMENTS IN THE MAILROOM. GO BACK TO THE MAILROOM AND SEE IF YOU CAN FIND THESE PROPS.
MOTORCYCLE HELMET
TAZER GLOVES
BINOCULARS
WALKIE-TALKIE
VIDEO MONITOR
LAPTOP COMPUTER
METAL BRIEFCASE
BOLT IS A VERY LONG WAY FROM HOME! HE BELONGS WITH PENNY IN CALIFORNIA. LOOK FOR THESE THINGS IN THE MOVING VAN THAT BELONG IN CALIFORNIA, TOO.
SUNGLASSES
SUNSCREEN
INNER TUBE
MEGAPHONE
VIDEO CAMERA
SURFBOARD
BEFORE BOLT GOT STUCK IN THE FENCE, HE RACED BETWEEN CARS ON THE STREETS OF NEW YORK CITY. GO BACK TO FIND THESE SIX YELLOW CABS STUCK IN TRAFFIC.

BOLT AND MITTENS SMELL LOTS OF DELICIOUS THINGS AT THE RV PARK. HEAD BACK TO FIND THESE FOODS THAT THEY MIGHT GET TO SAMPLE.
HOT DOG
CORN ON THE COB
SHISH KEBAB
HAMBURGER
SLICE OF PIZZA
ICE CREAM CONE
TURKEY DRUMSTICK
BOLT STAYS FOCUSED WHENEVER HE'S ON A MISSION. BUT THE DOGS IN THE POUND ARE EASILY DISTRACTED BY THINGS LIKE HAMSTERS AND DOGGIE TREATS. GO BACK TO THE POUND AND LOOK FOR TEN DELICIOUS DOG BONES.
AS THE CAST AND CREW EVACUATE THE SOUNDSTAGE, SOME THINGS GET LEFT BEHIND. LOOK FOR THESE THINGS THAT FELL BENEATH THE FEET OF THE CROWD.
TELEVISION SCRIPT
BOTTLE OF WATER
MAGAZINE
MOTORCYCLE HELMET
BOLT CLAPBOARD
BASEBALL CAP
RETURN TO THE FARMHOUSE TO LOOK FOR THESE PHOTOS OF BOLT AND HIS FAMILY.

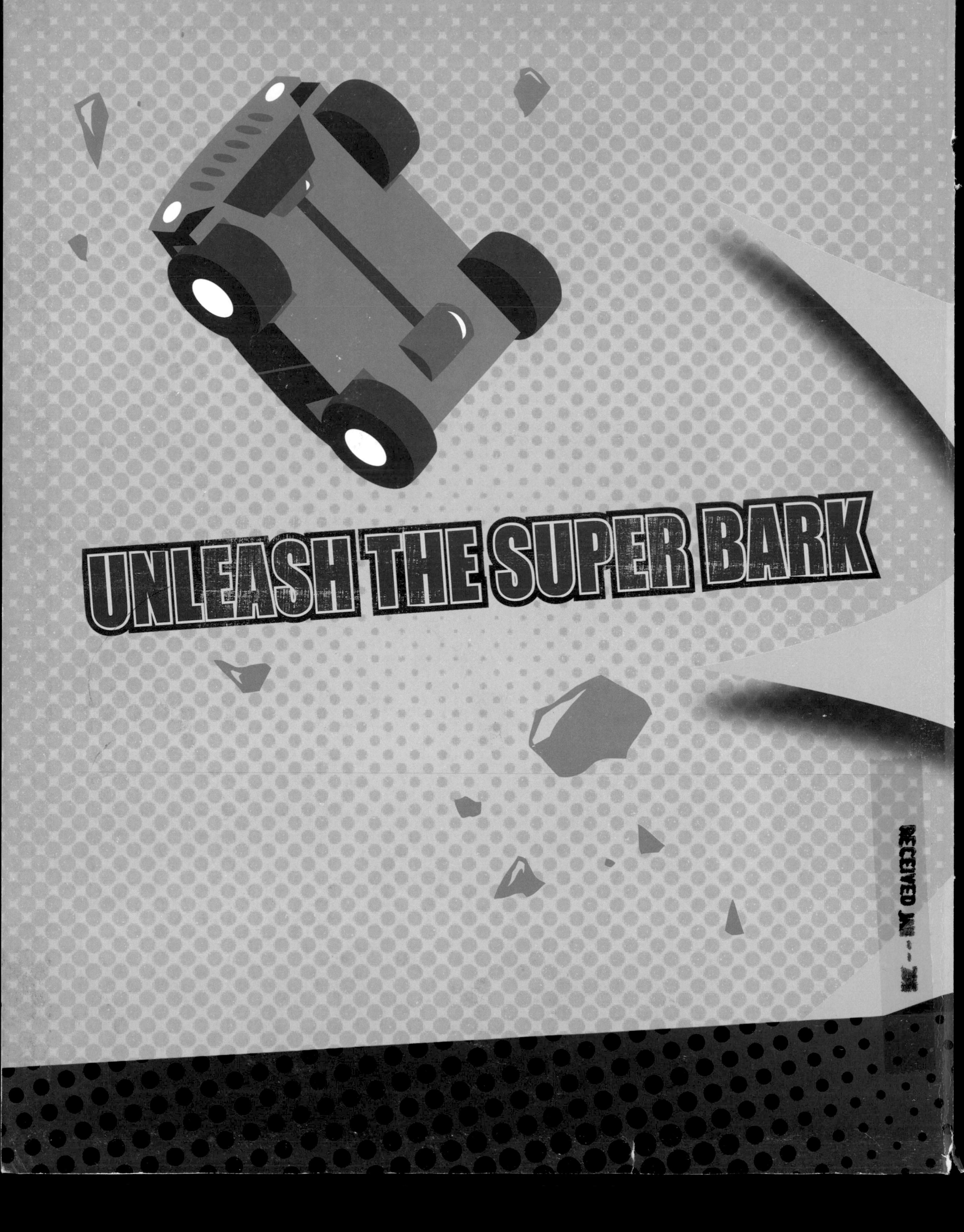
UNLEASH THE SUPER BARK